МЕЛЬНИЦА ПАХОМА
И ЕГО ЖЕНЫ

МЕЛЬНИЦА
ИВАНА

ВОЛГА

How Much Land
Does A Man Need?

First published in 2002 by

CROCODILE BOOKS
An imprint of Interlink Publishing Group, Inc.
99 Seventh Avenue • Brooklyn, New York 11215 and
46 Crosby Street • Northampton, Massachusetts 01060
www.interlinkbooks.com

Copyright © Speer Verlag AG, Zürich 1994, 2002
English Language Edition copyright © Crocodile Books 2002

Library of Congress Cataloging-in-Publication Data available
ISBN 1-56656-407-7

Printed and bound in Korea

How Much Land Does A Man Need?

by Leo Tolstoy
illustrated by Elena Abesinova

Crocodile Books, USA

An imprint of Interlink Publishing Group, Inc.

New York • Northampton

www.interlinkbooks.com

There were once two sisters who lived in Russia. The older sister married a merchant who lived in the city. The younger sister married a peasant who lived in the village. When the older sister visited the younger one, she boasted: "My life in the city is very good, much better than yours. I live in a big, beautiful house. Everything is clean, and I can eat and drink whatever I want. I can go out for pleasant rides and to the theater."

The younger sister defended her life in the country. "It's true that life here is not as beautiful or clean as it is for you. We must work hard. But our life is quiet and secure. The earth never fails to feed us, while you could lose everything tomorrow. There are great temptations in the city. Your husband could start drinking or gambling. He could find a lover. No such nonsense would ever cross my husband's mind. He has to work too hard."

Pakhom, the younger sister's husband, was lying near the fire. He heard what his wife was saying and thought to himself, *She's right. Every word she says is true. It's a shame about one thing, though. We have too little land. If we had more land, I would fear nothing and no one.*

The landowner in their village had always lived peacefully with the peasants. But when she hired a manager, he began to cause problems for everyone. If a cow wandered onto the landowner's property, the manager charged a fine. Pakhom often had to pay these fines. What little money he had saved was quickly used up. Soon he became ill-tempered and impatient with his family.

Eventually the landowner sold her property to the peasants. Pakhom watched with envy as his neighbor bought fifty acres of land. He said to his wife, "All the neighbors are buying land. We must buy some as well."

So Pakhom and his wife borrowed money from their brother-in-law who lived in the city. Pakhom's son had to hire himself out to the other peasants. But Pakhom managed to buy a twenty-five acre piece of land with a small stand of birch trees on it.

Pakhom was overjoyed. Now he was his own master. The grain stood tall. He had a bountiful harvest, and he made a handsome profit at market. He was able to repay all his debts. There was peace and happiness under his roof.

But this did not last for long. The neighbor's cows would often wander onto his land and eat until they were full. Pakhom asked the peasants to look after their cattle. But they didn't. So he took two of his neighbors to court to make them pay fines. They became angry, and damaged Pakhom's land on purpose. One morning, Pakhom found that his lovely little birch trees had all been knocked down and stripped of their bark. He was both heartbroken and furious.

He suspected his neighbor Simon had done it. So he took Simon to court. But Pakhom had no proof, and the judges let Simon go. Then Pakhom started quarreling with the judges. Soon everyone in the village was angry at him. It became very unpleasant for him to live there.

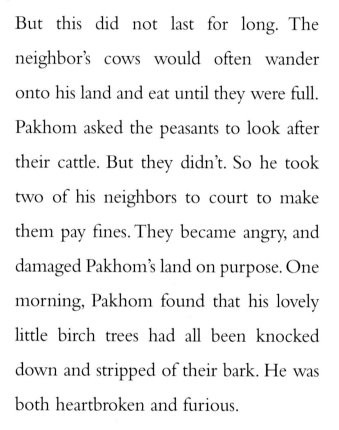

One evening, a traveling peasant asked for a resting place for the night. Pakhom welcomed him. During supper, the peasant said, "I come from the Lower Volga, where I have been working. There's a lot of good land there. You can buy it cheap. Many people from my village have moved there. And they have all become rich." Then Pakhom thought, *Why should I suffer here, when it could be so much better in the Volga?*

In the fall, Pakhom set off. He wanted to see for himself if everything was really as the stranger had said. And it was. So Pakhom returned home and sold his land and his farm, making a good profit. In the spring, he moved with his family to the Volga.

There, Pakhom and his family received a warm welcome. Pakhom gave generous gifts of food and drink to the elders of the village. In return, they helped him take care of all the necessary papers. Since Pakhom had a family of five, he was given one hundred twenty-five acres of land—five times as much land as he had had before. He immediately started to settle in. He bought cattle, plowed his fields, and everything went well. And yet, after a while he started feeling dissatisfied once again.

Pakhom's fields were spread apart. For a good harvest, he needed to keep moving his crops onto fresh land, which was difficult to do. He noticed that the rich farmers' homes stood right in the middle of their fields. And he thought: *If I could buy myself some more land, I would build my house like that.*

Then he heard of a farmer who was going through hard times. Pakhom arranged to buy twelve hundred acres of land from him for one thousand rubles. But shortly before the deal was settled, a traveling merchant asked Pakhom for a resting place for the night.

The merchant told Pakhom, "I come from the faraway Bashkir country. People there are very friendly. They have so much land that you need a whole year to walk around it. I brought them gifts, and they sold me twelve thousand acres for one thousand rubles. It's good, fertile land, and there's a river nearby." Pakhom thought to himself, *Why should I pay one thousand rubles for twelve hundred acres of land here if I can get ten times as much land for the same price there?*

Pakhom asked how to get to the Bashkir country. He wanted to travel there immediately. So he left his wife in charge of the farm and took a servant with him, stopping in the city to buy gifts. It took Pakhom and his servant many days to reach the Baskhirs' camp. But when they arrived, they received a very friendly welcome. The Bashkirs are a happy, carefree people. They don't plow their fields. Their cattle and horse herds are allowed to roam freely. The Bashkirs invited Pakhom into a tent and seated him on soft cushions and rugs. They fed him generously with fine cheeses and lamb and gave him tea to drink. Then Pakhom distributed his gifts. The Bashkirs were delighted. They said, "You have been so generous. Now tell us what we can do for you."

Pakhom said, "I would like to buy land from you. Back at home, the soil is exhausted, and it's too cramped for me. But here the land is good and wide."

The Bashkirs nodded and said, "To thank you for your friendliness, we shall give you as much land as you want." But then they started arguing among themselves. "We have no right to give away any land without our elder's approval," said one group. "Oh yes, we can," said the other.

While the Bashkirs argued, a man wearing a fox-fur cap came into the tent. He was the elder. He wanted to know the reason for the dispute. Pakhom gave him a gift of the most beautiful caftan and five pounds of tea. The elder told Pakhom, "If you want land, take as much as you can. We have enough." Pakhom thanked him and asked about the price.

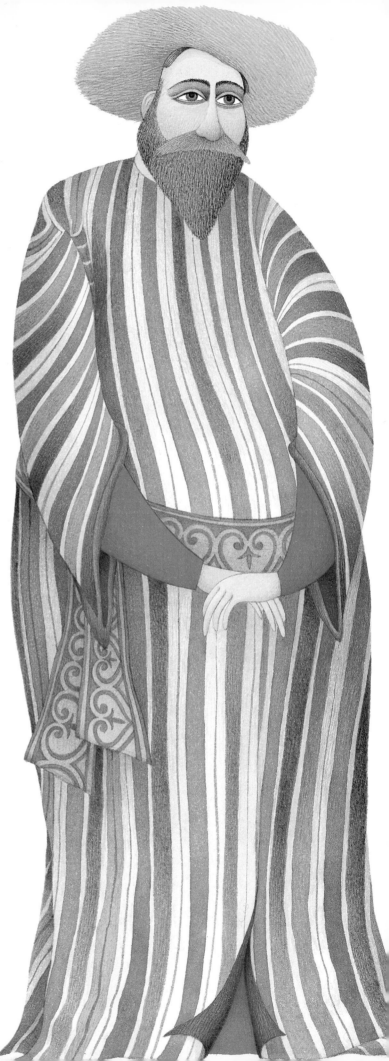

"We have only one price," said the elder. "That is one thousand rubles for the day." Pakhom didn't understand what he meant. So the elder explained, "You may have all the land you can walk around in one day. And the cost is one thousand rubles."

Astounded, Pakhom said, "But I can walk around a very big piece of land in a day."

The elder laughed, "Yes, and it's all yours. But come evening, you must be back at the place where you started. Otherwise, the land won't be yours. And we'll keep your money all the same."

Pakhom agreed to the deal. They decided that Pakhom would set off the following morning to walk around the land.

Pakhom went to him and asked, "What are you laughing at?" Then suddenly it was the merchant who was sitting there. And Pakhom asked him, "Have you been here long?"

But then it was the peasant from the Volga. Suddenly Pakhom saw a dead body lying on the ground, and realized in horror that the body was his. He immediately woke up and tried to shake off the nightmare. Then he woke up his servant and the Bashkirs. "Come on, let's go," said Pakhom. "It's time for me to walk around my land. The sun will soon be up."

That night Pakhom lay down, but he could not sleep. He calculated that in such a long summer day, he could well walk fifty miles. And he pictured everything he would do with all this land. "I'll lease the poorer land and keep the better for myself. Then I'll buy two yokes of oxen and hire two more servants."

Just before dawn, he fell asleep and dreamed. He saw the elder of the Bashkirs sitting outside the tent, laughing out loud.

The Bashkirs rode with Pakhom to a hill. Looking out over the land, the elder said to Pakhom, "All this land belongs to us. Now choose a piece for yourself." Pakhom's eyes burned with desire. The elder put his fox-fur cap on the ground. "This is your mark. You'll start from here, and this is where you must return. If you aren't back by sunset, you will have lost the deal. If you are back, then all the land that you have walked around shall be yours."

Pakhom put his money on the cap. Then he took off his caftan and waited for the first ray of sun.

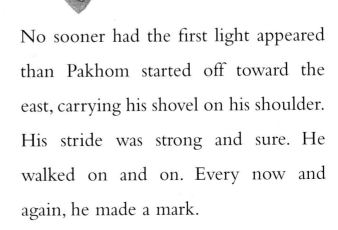

No sooner had the first light appeared
than Pakhom started off toward the
east, carrying his shovel on his shoulder.
His stride was strong and sure. He
walked on and on. Every now and
again, he made a mark.

Now he had to turn to walk the second side of the square. He grew tired, and the sun was scorching. Pakhom allowed himself only a short lunch break, eating and drinking just a little. "I must not rest, otherwise I'll fall asleep," he said to himself. Then he went on his way.

After a few hours, Pakhom told himself: "It's still too early to turn. The soil here is so good. The longer I walk, the better the land I will have." And in his greed, he went on walking. He was drenched in sweat. When he looked back toward the place from where he had started, it seemed as tiny as an anthill.

He walked a long distance on this side of the square as well. Every time he wanted to turn, a beautiful spot would lure him, or a fresh meadow would beckon. Finally he turned into the third side of the square. He saw that the first two sides were far too long. So he doubled his step. The third side would have to be shorter.

It was nearing sunset. Pakhom began to panic. What if he didn't reach the starting point in time? He turned into the fourth side of the square. There were now some fifteen miles between himself and the cap. He started running, straight toward the hill.

Pakhom ran and ran. The cap was still so far away, and he was tired. His feet ached and were covered with blisters and scratches. "I must hurry," he urged himself. "I've walked too far. If I'm late, I'll lose both the land and my money." With one last effort, he forced himself to go faster and faster. He was panting, his heart was pounding, and his mouth was dry. The sun was deep on the horizon. Pakhom ran even faster. At long last, he reached the foot of the hill. The sun was sinking. "Alas," he moaned, "I won't reach the goal. Everything is lost, and I'm ruined."

Then he heard the Bashkirs call. They waved to him and urged him on. At the top of the hill, the sun was still visible. With his last ounce of strength, Pakhom rushed up the hillside. The elder sat there, and he was indeed laughing out loud. Pakhom groaned. His legs collapsed beneath him. His hands just managed to reach the cap.

Then the elder shouted, "Well done! You have won a lot of land." But Pakhom couldn't hear him, for he had fallen down dead. The Bashkirs were deeply saddened. Pakhom's servant took the shovel and dug his master a grave—just as long and as wide as Pakhom's body where it lay upon the earth.

LEO TOLSTOY

1828–1910

Leo Tolstoy is one of the world's most famous writers. His best known works are *War and Peace, Anna Karenina*, and *Resurrection*. He wrote countless stories and novellas. His later years were dedicated to religious and political writings.

Lev (Leo) Nikolayevich Tolstoy was the second youngest of the five children of Nikolay Ilich Tolstoy and a rich prince's daughter, Maria Volkonskaya. He was born on August 28, 1828, on the family estate, Yasnaya Polyana (Gov. Tula, Central Russia). His parents died early, and an aunt came to Yasnaya to look after Leo and his brothers and sisters. Like all children born into Russian landed aristocracy, they were educated at home, and enjoyed a carefree country life.

Later, Tolstoy studied law at the Kazan University. He cut his studies short after three years and retired to the Yasnaya estate, which he was to inherit. He wanted to be a progressive landowner, and had many new ideas he wanted to put in place to improve the life of his serfs. But these changes were met with incomprehension by the serfs, and in disappointment, Tolstoy went to Moscow.

In 1851, he and his brother joined the Russian army and went to the Caucasus. There Tolstoy discovered the simple life of the Cossacks, which he later depicted in his stories. At the end of 1854, he participated in the defense of Sebastopol in the famous Fourth Crimean Bastion. His three war tales about Sebastopol made him famous througout the country.

After leaving the army in 1856, Tolstoy went back to his estate. He was willing to grant freedom to his serfs, but was again defeated by their mistrust. Following an extended European journey, he opened a school for the peasants' children on his estate, where he taught according to modern, anti-authoritarian methods.

In 1862, he married Sophia Andreyevna Bers, a doctor's daughter who bore him thirteen children. Yet their marriage was not always happy. In the second half of his life, Tolstoy neglected literature and devoted himself to religion. He turned away from the church and developed his own faith. Rejecting all worldly possessions, he put his estate in his wife's name, and in 1901 he even refused the Nobel Prize.

In 1878, the writer Ivan Turgenev visited Tolstoy and tried to urge him to go back to his writing. From his deathbed in 1883, Turgenev wrote Tolstoy a letter, admonishing "the great writer of the Russian land" to return to literature. In 1884, Tolstoy resumed his literary work while still continuing his religious activities. He set up a publishing house with a plan to publish good, inexpensive books.

In 1891, Tolstoy renounced his literary copyrights. Sophia, thinking of their many children, failed to understand this, and fought to retain some of the copyrights, thus securing at least part of the children's education. But the differences between Tolstoy and Sophia remained. On the night of October 28, 1910, Tolstoy left the estate of Yasnaya Polyana. A few days later, on November 7, the internationally celebrated writer died of a lung infection.

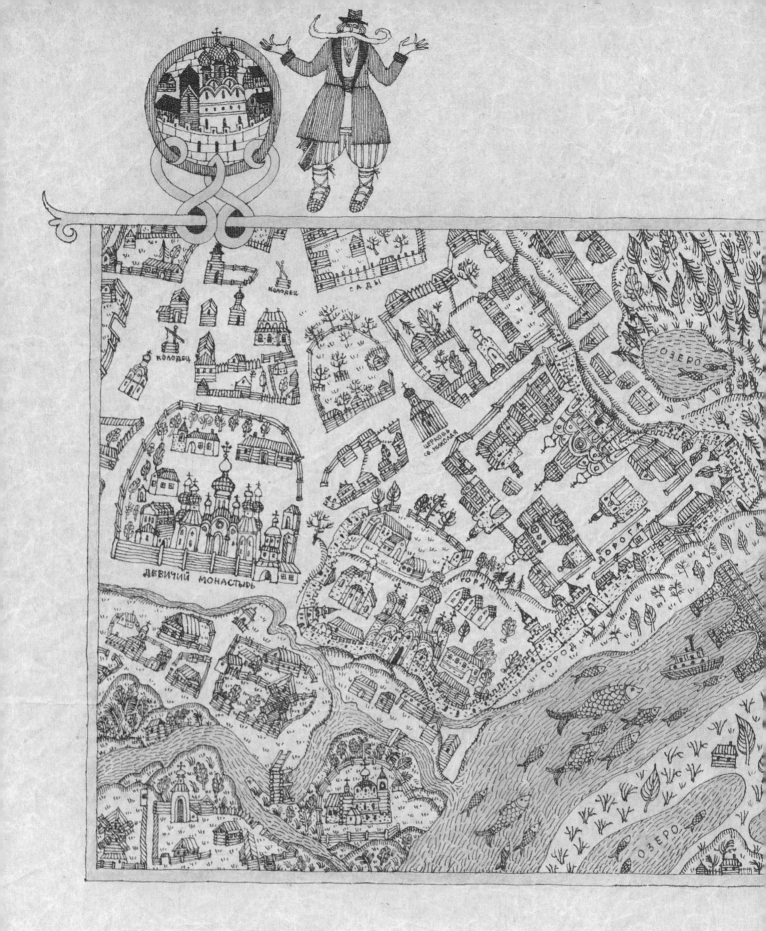